274685

There's a Cow

Ca ch

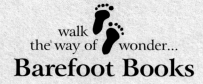

walk
the way of wonder...
Barefoot Books

There's a cow in the cabbage patch, moo, moo, moo!

She should be in the dairy, what shall we do?

There's a dove in the dairy, coo, coo, coo!

He should be in the dovecote, what shall we do?

There's an owl in the dovecote, t-wit, t-wit, t-woo!

He should be in the old barn, what shall we do?

There's a horse in the old barn, and a donkey, too!

They should be in the stable, what shall we do?

There's a rooster in the stable, cock-a-doodle-doo!

He should be in the henhouse, what shall we do?

There's a pig in the henhouse, with piglets pink and new.

They should be in the pigsty, what shall we do?

There's a black sheep in the pigsty, with lambs one and two.

They should be in the meadow, what shall we do?

dairy

henhouse

stabl

meadow

barn

pigsty

dovecote

**Tell them all it's dinnertime, then it won't be long
'til all these naughty animals are back where they belong!**

Praise for Clare Beaton

How Big is a Pig?
'Bold, bright tableaux...a sassy, unexpected wrap-up; Beaton will have her audience's attention all sewn up' — *Publishers Weekly, US*

Mother Goose Remembers
'She exquisitely and inventively crafts each picture' — *Publishers Weekly, US*

One Moose, Twenty Mice
'Clare Beaton's dazzlingly colourful felt work provides a splendid pictorial counting base in her number book' — *Carousel*

Zoë and her Zebra
'A useful teaching tool which is highly attractive' — *Early Years Educator*

For Annabel and Benedict – S. B.
For Gavin, who is frightened of cows – C. B.

Barefoot Books
PO Box 95
Kingswood
Bristol
BS30 5BH

Text copyright © 2001 by Stella Blackstone
Illustrations copyright © 2001 by Clare Beaton
The moral right of Stella Blackstone to be identified as the author and Clare Beaton
to be identified as the illustrator of this work has been asserted

First published in Great Britain in 2001 by Barefoot Books Ltd
All rights reserved. No part of this book may be reproduced in any form or by any means,
electronic or mechanical, including photocopying, recording or by any information storage
and retrieval system, without permission in writing from the publisher

This book was typeset in Plantin Schoolbook Bold 20 on 28 point
The illustrations were prepared in felt with beads and buttons

Graphic design by Judy Linard, London
Colour transparencies by Jonathan Fisher Photography, Bath
Colour separation by Grafiscan, Verona
Printed and bound in Singapore by Tien Wah Press Pte Ltd

This book has been printed on 100% acid-free paper

Hardback ISBN 1 84148 332 X
Paperback ISBN 1 84148 334 6

British Cataloguing-in-Publication Data: a catalogue record for this book is available from the British Library

1 3 5 7 9 8 6 4 2